This book belongs to

....

....

Written by Katherine Sully
Illustrated by Emma Leach

Squeak the Lion

Little Squeak was the youngest lion cub in the pride.
All the other lions loved Squeak.

"He's so cute and cuddly," they said.

"Isn't he funny?" they said.

But Squeak didn't want to be cute or funny. Squeak wanted to be just like his older brothers, Bruno and Leo.

Bruno was brave and strong.

Leo was clever and cunning.

Squeak wasn't even his proper name. His real name was Rory. That was a proper lion's name. Squeak was a silly, baby name.

"Why does everyone call me Squeak?" he asked his brothers grumpily.

"Because when you were a baby, you went *Squeak!*" explained Leo.

"So everyone called you Squeak!" laughed Bruno.

One day, Bruno and Leo were going hunting.
"Wait for me!" called Squeak, trotting after them.
Squeak hurried to catch up, but soon his little legs
were feeling tired.

He stopped for a rest and
watched as Bruno and
Leo disappeared into the
tall grass.

When he finally caught up with them, Bruno and Leo were crouched over a nest of tasty-looking eggs. Suddenly, there was a HISSsss!

A head appeared, swaying above the tall grass — it was a snake! The nest of eggs belonged to her. She lunged at the lion cubs. But brave Bruno roared. He swiped the snake with his paw, and it slithered away.

"Wow, Bruno, that was brave!" said Leo, as the lion cubs made their way home.

"Did you see how Bruno swiped that sneaky snake?" said Squeak. Just at that moment, Squeak spotted a lizard crossing the path. He swiped the lizard with his paw, just like Bruno. But the lizard quickly flicked out its tongue, smacking Squeak on the nose.

Squeak was so surprised that he jumped. The angry
lizard continued on his way.

Bruno and Leo laughed. "You're so funny, Squeak!"
they roared.

The next day, Bruno and Leo went hunting again.

"Wait for me!" called Squeak, as he followed his brothers down to the watering hole. It was very muddy along the bank, and Squeak's paws kept sinking into the mud. It slowed him down.

"Now I'll never catch up," he sighed as he watched his brothers walking ahead.

Then, Bruno and Leo stopped. They had
spied some paw prints in the mud.
   "These tracks belong to a water buffalo," said clever
Leo, sniffing the ground.
   "Let's follow it and sneak up on it from behind,"
said brave Bruno, as he looked along the
muddy trail.

By the time Squeak reached the water, there were lots of paw prints in the mud. And his brothers were nowhere to be seen. Squeak sniffed the ground and looked at the paw prints.

"I can follow tracks, too," said Squeak to himself, and then he set off. He followed the tracks around. . .

and around. . .

for a long way. . .

until. . .

Squeak could hear his
brothers laughing. He looked
up, then looked around
at the tracks. Squeak had
followed his own tracks in
a big circle!

"You're so funny, Squeak!"
laughed Bruno and Leo.

The following day, Bruno and Leo were going
hunting again.

"Wait for me!" called Squeak. But this time, his brothers
didn't want Squeak to come along.

"Not this time, Squeak," said Bruno. "You'll slow
us down."

"Or get into trouble," said Leo.

But Squeak wasn't going to miss a hunting trip! He
followed his brothers a little way behind.

Bruno and Leo soon disappeared down a trail through some trees. They followed the trail until they found a good place to set a trap. Clever Leo piled up some berries under a tree where a hungry squirrel would find them. Brave Bruno climbed up the tree and crept along a branch, ready to pounce.

Very soon, a squirrel hopped toward the berries. The trap had worked! Bruno crept further along the branch, ready to pounce. But, suddenly, there was a **CRACK!** The branch came crashing down. The startled squirrel ran off as Bruno tumbled to the ground.

"OUCH!" roared Bruno. His tail was caught under the branch. Bruno was trapped — he couldn't move!

"Don't worry, Bruno!" called clever Leo. "I'll find a way to get you out."

Squeak had just caught up with his brothers
and was watching from behind a tree.

"Oh, my tail!" Bruno moaned. "Hurry up,
and help me out."

"Now," thought Leo, "all I need is a vine
and a heavy rock to lift the branch. . ."

But Leo didn't finish because a loud HARUMPH interrupted him.
It was the sound of an elephant.

"Oh, no!" groaned Bruno. "We're on an elephant trail!"

"And the elephants are heading this way!" gasped Leo.

While Leo dashed about to find a piece of rope, a long line of elephants appeared at the end of the track. Squeak looked at the elephants, then looked at Bruno trapped under the branch.

The elephants were getting nearer and nearer. Leo wasn't going to make it in time. The ground began to shake as the elephants trampled closer and closer.

"There's no time to lose," thought Squeak. He saw a gap below the branch that was just big enough for him to squeeze under. He dashed out from his hiding place. . . into the gap, and with more of a ROAR than a squeak. . . he heaved the branch with all his might.

The branch lifted just enough for Bruno to pull out his tail.
Then, Squeak pulled the branch away. The elephants were
almost on top of them.

Bruno, Squeak and Leo leapt into the trees just as the elephants came thundering by.

"Wow, Squeak, that was brave!" said Bruno.

"That was really clever, Squeak!" said Leo.

The three brothers climbed down from the tree.
"Did you see the way Squeak came to the rescue?"
said Bruno.

"Wait until we tell everyone how brave and clever
Squeak was!" said Leo.

Squeak felt very proud. "Maybe we should
call you Rory from now on," said his brothers.

Squeak smiled. But somehow, he didn't mind being called Squeak anymore.